This book belongs to ...

....

Tips for Talking and Reading Together

Stories are an enjoyable and reassuring way of introducing children to new experiences.

Before you read the story:

- Talk about the title and the picture on the cover. Ask your child what they think the story might be about.
- Talk about what happens on a farm. Has your child ever been to a farm with you? Is there a farm near your house?

Read the story with your child. After you have read the story:

- Discuss the Talk About ideas on page 27.
- Go through the Story of Milk on pages 28 – 29.
- Do the fun activity on page 30.

Have fun!

Find the ten sparrows hidden in the pictures.

Fun at the Farm

Written by Roderick Hunt and Annemarie Young
Illustrated by Nick Schon,
based on the original characters
created by Alex Brychta

OXFORD

UNIVERSITY PRESS

Kipper's class was going to spend a day at a farm.

"Farmers produce food for us to eat," said Miss Green.

"We get our eggs from chickens," she said,
"and our milk from cows. We get flour from wheat, and our
meat from animals."

5

The next day the class arrived at Farmer Gow's. Chris Gow met them.

"You're all going to be farmers for a day today," she said.

"First we'll feed the animals. You can all help me," said Chris.

"I hope we don't have to touch the animals," said Sam.

Chris took them into a barn with animal pens. One pen had a sheep and a lamb, one had a goat and a kid, and one had a cow and her calf.

The animals pushed their noses through the bars.
Anna and Kipper patted their heads, but Sam didn't
want to.

The animals jumped up and down. Kipper and Anna patted them. Sam didn't. He didn't like them pushing their noses into his hand.

"It's important to give animals the right food," said Chris.

"Not ice cream!" said Kipper.

Everyone laughed.

"We'll feed the lambs first," said Chris. "On this farm we feed milk to some of the lambs. Who wants to help?"

The children got into groups. Kipper, Anna and Sam were together. Chris gave each group a bottle of milk with a teat on the end.

Chris lifted a few of the lambs out of the pen. They ran to the children and began sucking at the bottles.

"They look hungry," said Anna.

Kipper and Anna took it in turns to feed the lamb, but Sam didn't want to.

"I'll just watch," he said.

Next, Chris gave the children special food to feed the lambs.

They fed milk
to the kids.

Then the children fed the sheep.

"Their lips tickle," laughed
Kipper.

Last of all they fed the calves.

"What long tongues!" said Anna.

Then they went to see the hens.

"Do they all lay eggs?" asked Sam.

"Yes, all of these do," said Chris.

"Can I collect eggs?" asked Sam.

Sam, Kipper and Anna each picked up an egg very carefully and handed it to Chris to put in a basket.

It was time for lunch, so they all washed their hands very carefully.

After lunch they went for a ride round the farm on a trailer.

They stopped to look at the cows.

"Cows drink a lot of water," said Chris. "As much as 25 bucketfuls of water a day."

After the trailer-ride the children played on the bale climb. The bales smelled of hay and there were tunnels inside them.

Kipper chased Anna up and down the bales. They pretended to be pirates.

"This is fun," said Kipper.

Soon it was time to go home.

"Where is Sam?" asked Miss Green.

"He wasn't on the bales," said Anna.

24

Kipper, Anna and Anna's dad went to look for Sam.

"He can't be far away," said Kipper.

"I went to say goodbye to the hens," said Sam.
"And Chris gave me an egg to take home!"

Talk about the story

What did the children do at the farm?

Why did the children wash their hands carefully before lunch?

How did Sam feel about the hens?

What is your favourite animal at the farm?

The story of milk

Cows have to be milked twice a day every day.

They go into a milking parlour. The farmer washes their udders.

Then the farmer uses a machine to suck out the milk.

The milk is pumped into a large glass or stainless steel tank.

It is cooled and stored until a tanker comes to collect it.

The raw milk is treated to make it safe.

Milk is put into cartons, or made into cheese, butter and yoghurt.

Baby animals

Match the baby animals to their mothers.

kid

calf

chick

foal

lamb

FIRST EXPERIENCES WITH Biff, Chip & Kipper

Have you read them all yet?

Kipper's First Pet

Learning to Swim

Going to the Dentist

Going to the Doctor

series created by Roderick Hunt and Alex Brychta

Going to the Hairdresser

Fun at the Farm

series created by Roderick Hunt and Alex Brychta

OXFORD

Going on a Plane

series created by Roderick Hunt and Alex Brychta

Starting School

series created by Roderick Hunt and Alex Brychta

OXFORD

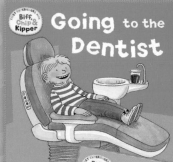

FIRST EXPERIENCES Flashcards
55 cards

Also available:
- **Kipper Gets Nits!**
- **At the Hospital**
- **At the Optician**
- **Bottles, Cans, Plastic Bags**
- **On a Train**
- **At the Vet**
- **At the Match**
- **At the Dance Class**

Read with Biff, Chip and Kipper
The UK's best-selling home reading series

Phonics

First Stories

	Phonics				First Stories			
Level 1 Getting ready to read	Kipper's Alphabet I Spy	Chip's Letter Sounds	Biff's Wonder Words	Floppy's Fun Phonics	Get On	Floppy Did This!	Up You Go	Six in a Bed
Level 2 Starting to read	I am Kipper	Cat in a Bag	The Red Hen	The Fizz-Buzz	Funny Fish	Silly Races!	The Snowman	Dad's Birthday
Level 3 Becoming a reader	Such a Fuss	Shops	The Sing Song	The Backpack	Poor Old Rabbit	I Can Trick a Tiger	Super Dad	Floppy and the Bone
Level 4 Developing as a reader	Wet Feet	The Moon Jet	The Red Goat	Quick! Quick!	Missing!	The Raft Race	Dragon Danger	The Spaceship
Level 5 Building confidence in reading	Egg Fried Rice	Craig Saves the Day	Seasick	Dolphin Rescue	Hungry Floppy	Husky Adventure	Trapped!	Looking after Gran
Level 6 Reading with confidence	Gran's New Blue Shoes	Ice City	Save Pudding Wood	Uncle Max	Hairy-Scary Monster	Mountain Rescue	The Lost Voice	Secret of the Sands

Phonics stories help children practise their sounds and letters, as they learn to do in school.

First stories have been specially written to provide practice in reading everyday language.

OXFORD
UNIVERSITY PRESS

Great Clarendon Street, Oxford OX2 6DP

Text © Roderick Hunt and Annemarie Young 2009

Illustrations © Alex Brychta and Nick Schon 2009

First published 2009

This edition published 2012

10 9 8 7 6 5 4 3 2

Series Editors: Kate Ruttle, Annemarie Young

British Library Cataloguing in Publication Data available

ISBN: 978-0-19-848797-5

Printed in China by Imago

The characters in this work are the original creation of Roderick Hunt and Alex Brychta who retain copyright in the characters.

With thanks to Anne Gow